To

....

From

....

First published in Great Britain by HarperCollins *Children's Books* in 2019

1 3 5 7 9 10 8 6 4 2

ISBN: 978-0-00-827354-5

HarperCollins *Children's Books* is a division of HarperCollins *Publishers* Ltd.

Text and illustrations copyright © HarperCollins *Publishers* Ltd 2019
Indigenous artwork on pages 6-7, *Dreaming Circles Contemporary*,
Dreaming Circles Traditional and *Yirraay – The Sun*, copyright © Gregg Dreise 2017

Visit our website at www.harpercollins.co.uk

Printed and bound in China

MIX
Paper from
responsible sources
FSC™ C007454

This book is produced from independently certified FSC™ paper
to ensure responsible forest management.
For more information visit: www.harpercollins.co.uk/green

Why I Love Australia

Illustrated by Daniel Howarth

HarperCollins *Children's Books*

I love Australia because...

the beaches are amazing.

I love Australia because...

we have the world's oldest
living indigenous culture.

I love Australia because...

we have one of the most
famous harbours ever.

I love Australia because...

there are sacred
and beautiful places.

I love Australia because...

we have the largest coral reef in the world.

I love Australia because...

there are over 150 'big things'.

I love Australia because...
Christmas is in the summer!

I love Australia because...

we have the oldest surviving
tropical rainforest in the world.

I love Australia because...
the snacks are yummy!

I love Australia because...
we have great ski fields!

I love Australia because...

holidays at home are so much fun!

I love Australia because...

we can play sport all year long.

I love Australia because...

the outback is awesome!

Everyone loves Australia, especially...

...ME!

Stick a picture of yourself

in Australia here.